The GHOST and MAX MONROE

CASE #3

THE DIRTY TRICK

the GHOST and MAX MONROE

CASE #3
THE DIRTY TRICK

WRITTEN BY **L.M. FALCONE**

ILLUSTRATIONS BY **KIM SMITH**

KIDS CAN PRESS

To kid detectives everywhere!

Text © 2015 L. M. Falcone
Illustrations © 2015 Kids Can Press

Kids Can Press acknowledges the financial support of the Government of Ontario, through the Ontario Media Development Corporation's Ontario Book Initiative; the Ontario Arts Council; the Canada Council for the Arts; and the Government of Canada, through the CBF, for our publishing activity.

Published in Canada by
Kids Can Press Ltd.
25 Dockside Drive
Toronto, ON M5A 0B5

Published in the U.S. by
Kids Can Press Ltd.
2250 Military Road
Tonawanda, NY 14150

www.kidscanpress.com

Edited by Yasemin Uçar and Katie Scott
Designed by Marie Bartholomew
Illustrations by Kim Smith
Chapter icon illustrations by Andrew Dupuis

The hardcover edition of this book is smyth sewn casebound.
The paperback edition of this book is limp sewn with a drawn-on cover.
Manufactured in Malaysia in 3/2015 by Tien Wah Press (Pte.) Ltd.

CM 15 0 9 8 7 6 5 4 3 2 1
CM PA 15 0 9 8 7 6 5 4 3 2 1

Library and Archives Canada Cataloguing in Publication

Falcone, L. M. (Lucy M.), 1951–, author
   The ghost and Max Monroe. Case #3, The dirty trick /
written by L. M. Falcone ; illustrations by Kim Smith.

(The ghost and Max Monroe)
ISBN 978-1-77138-155-0 (bound)   ISBN 978-1-77138-019-5 (pbk.)

I. Smith, Kim, 1986–, illustrator II. Title. III. Title: Dirty trick.

PS8561.A574G464 2015   jC813'.6   C2014-906918-9

Kids Can Press is a *Corus*™ Entertainment company

CONTENTS

Prologue 7

Chapter 1 9

Chapter 2 19

Chapter 3 33

Chapter 4 39

Chapter 5 46

Chapter 6 54

Chapter 7 67

Chapter 8 72

Chapter 9 77

Chapter 10 84

PROLOGUE

Max sat down beside his grandfather. "Your brother, Larry, is a *ghost?*"

"Yup."

"And he *haunts* the detective agency in the backyard?"

"Yup." Harry shot some whipped cream into his mouth. "Sometimes he hangs around the house. But mostly, he sits in the coach house, bawling his eyes out."

"I heard crying!"

"That'd be Larry. He likes to have a good cry around this time of day."

Max shook his head. "Crying ghosts … haunted detective agencies … I'll wake up any minute and everything will be normal."

CHAPTER 1

DON'T WAIT UP!

Max Monroe couldn't believe his luck.
His grandpa Harry had made his favorite
supper twice in one week — lasagna with
cheesy garlic bread. Max remembered that
it was his dad's favorite meal, too, and he
suddenly missed him. Max's father was
a reporter sent on overseas assignments.
He'd been away since the beginning of the
summer and wouldn't be home for a while.

Harry scraped his plate clean. "Delicious!
I *love* lasagna!"

Max smiled. "Me, too."

Harry wiped his mouth with a napkin. "Hate to eat and run, but it's bowling night — and tonight's the big tournament!"

He got up and rushed out of the kitchen.

Max cleared the dishes. Suddenly, he spotted a light passing by the dark window. A few seconds later, the light passed by again, and then again. Finally, his great-uncle Larry floated through the open window holding a flashlight. Max was still getting used to the idea of having a ghost around. He put a plate in the sink and asked, "Any luck finding the dog?"

"Zip." Larry sounded annoyed. "I'll bet my last dollar that dumb mutt doesn't even exist."

"Then who's eating all the dog food?"

"How do I know?" Larry slumped down in a chair.

For over a week now, Max's uncle Larry had been on a quest to actually *see* the dog that pooped all over the yard and ate every morsel of food Grandpa Harry put out. So far, no luck.

Larry noticed two boxes of Mighty Moe's Donuts on the counter. He sprang up, lifted both lids and peered inside. "Where'd all these donuts come from?"

"Grandpa had a coupon — buy one, get one free."

Larry laughed. "Harry never could resist a bargain. When we were kids, he bought us each a pair of snowshoes because they were on sale. Trouble was — we lived in Florida!"

A car horn honked.

Harry scurried through the kitchen. "That's Claddie! But I can't for the *life* of me remember where I put my ball. Max, if you were a bowling ball, where would I put you?"

"In the fridge," said Max.

"The fridge?"

"You said bowling balls roll better when they're cold."

Harry's face lit up. "That's right!"

He pulled open the fridge door and lifted out his bowling ball. "Don't wait up!" he shouted over his shoulder as he rushed out the door.

SPOOKY MYSTERIES

Max finished doing the dishes then headed into the backyard. Sometimes at night he liked to read *Starchy* comics that his uncle Larry stashed away in the detective agency. As he waded through the tall grass, he thought about all the years that Larry had been a detective and how he hadn't solved one single case. Now, in the short time since Max had come to stay with his grandfather, he and Larry had solved *two* mysteries. They'd found a missing zucchini *and* a girl who disappeared during a magic trick.

Things were looking up.

As Max neared the detective agency, he heard the phone ring.

"Phone!" shouted Larry, streaking past him. In a flash, he was inside the office.

Max climbed through the window. The key to the detective agency had been missing for years.

Larry picked up the phone. With a cheery voice he said, "Monroe Detective Agency."

"I *really* need your help!" said a woman on the other end of the line. "A note has been slipped into my purse. It says, *Beware ... a dirty trick!*"

Larry covered the mouthpiece and whispered, "Max! A note that says *Beware ... a dirty trick!* has been slipped into someone's purse!"

"Into whose purse?" asked Max.

"I don't know."

"Ask?" suggested Max.

Larry nodded. "May I ask who's calling, please?"

"My name is Rhonda Remington. I write mystery books."

Larry covered the mouthpiece again. "Rhonda Remington. She writes mysteries."

Max's eyes opened wide. "Rhonda *Remington*? Grandpa and I have been reading her spooky mysteries. She's *great*." He grabbed the phone. "Hello? Miss Remington? This is Max Monroe."

SICK WITH WORRY

"Max, I'm so glad you're there," said Rhonda.

Max frowned. "Have we met?"

"No, but the gentleman at the front desk suggested you might be able to help. He'd read an article about the Monroe Detective Agency. He found the newspaper and noticed the agency's number was listed in the article."

"There's something the article didn't mention," said Max.

"What's that?"

"I'm ten."

Larry's eyes bugged out. *"Why are you telling her that?!"*

"Ten years old?" asked Rhonda.

"Uh-huh," replied Max. There was a long silence on the other end of the line.

Max watched Larry pace back and forth, wringing his hands. He knew that his uncle desperately wanted another case — and another chance to redeem his reputation. Being called a bumbling detective when he was alive had left a dark mark on Larry's heart.

"I thought you sounded a little young," said Rhonda. "But the young man who programs my computer isn't much older than you, and he's an absolute genius! So, I don't mind."

"That's great, Miss Remington."

Larry's face lit up. He leaned in to listen on the line.

"I've been nominated for the Mystery Hall of Fame," Rhonda continued. "One person is inducted every year, and the ceremony is tonight after a reception. I'm calling from Waldon Hall — do you know where that is?"

Max looked at Larry. Larry nodded his head.

"Yes," said Max.

"I know this is short notice, but can you meet me here tonight? Since I got that note, I've been *sick* with worry. I'd hate for anyone to play a dirty trick on me when I'm so close to receiving this great honor."

Max couldn't believe one of his favorite authors needed *his* help. "I'm on my way."

CHAPTER 2

GHOSTS GO TO THE MOVIES

As Max hung up the phone, he noticed Larry frowning.

"What's wrong, Uncle Larry?"

"Rhonda Remington needs our help tonight, and I can't go."

"Why not?"

"I promised Gertrude Finklestein I'd take her to the movies — a Three Stooges marathon. She used to date Curly, you know."

"Who's Gertrude Finklestein?" asked Max.

"A lady friend."

"A *ghost* lady friend? I didn't know ghosts go to the movies."

"Why wouldn't we?"

Max shook his head. He still had so much to learn about ghosts.

"You *can't* take this case without me," cried Larry. "We're a team — like Sherlock and Watson, Abbott and Costello, peanut butter and jelly."

Max slipped on his detective coat and tucked his notebook into the pocket. "Sorry, Uncle Larry, but Miss Remington is in trouble and she needs my help. I've gotta go."

Larry crossed his arms. "And just *how* do you plan on getting to Waldon Hall?"

Max thought for a moment. "If you give

me a ride, I'll give you my share of the donuts."

"Deal!" said Larry.

While Larry got the motorcycle, Max scribbled a note to his grandpa Harry. He left it on the kitchen table and dashed out the door.

THE WALLS HAVE EARS

Larry and Max drove to the outskirts of town. They arrived at a dark wooded area and continued up a winding hill.

"Spooky," said Larry.

At the top of the hill stood Waldon Hall. It was an old-fashioned three-story stone building surrounded by large oak trees. Cobblestones led up to the main doors. Larry's motorcycle roared through the open gates, zoomed up the driveway and screeched to a stop in the parking lot. Max hung on tightly to keep from flying out of the sidecar.

"Now, Max," said Larry, sliding off the bike, "you're on your own tonight, and I won't be there to help you. But if you stay *focused*, everything will be okay."

Max smiled when he heard this advice. His uncle Larry was the most *un*focused person he had ever met.

Max stepped out of the sidecar and took off his helmet. "Stay focused. Got it."

"Ask questions … study all the clues … and be very *observant*."

"I will, Uncle Larry."

Larry didn't need to look human once he was off his motorcycle, so he slipped out of his long coat, aviator's cap and goggles. After stashing his disguise in the sidecar, he told Max he would pick him up after the movie. Then he gave a thumbs-up and disappeared.

Max headed into Waldon Hall. A crowd of people stood around the lobby talking. As Max made his way through the room, he noticed gold-framed portraits running along one wall. In the middle of the room was a round table with a sign that read, *Mystery Hall of Fame — Competition Night.* Max spotted an information desk to his right and walked up to a bushy-haired man with big eyes who was reading a newspaper.

"My name is Max Monroe. Can you tell me where I can find Rhonda Remington?"

A round-faced lady with curly brown hair

was standing nearby. When she heard Max say his name, she hurried over, grabbed his hand and walked him away from the desk. "We can't talk here," she whispered. "The walls have ears."

THE CASE BEGINS

The lady led Max through an emergency exit and into the stairwell.

"Hello, Max. I'm Rhonda Remington." She turned and made sure the door was firmly closed. "Thanks for coming on such short notice." Rhonda took a folded note out of her pocket. "Here's the note that someone slipped into my purse."

Max looked at the note. It was neatly written in blue ink on plain white paper and read:

Beware ... a dirty trick!

"Do you recognize the handwriting, Miss Remington?"

"I'm afraid not."

"It looks like someone's trying to warn you."

"Yes, but who? And why wouldn't they just tell me in person? And what *kind* of dirty trick do they mean?"

"That's what I'm here to find out," said Max.

The steps in the stairwell below them creaked.

"Shhh," said Rhonda. "Someone's coming."

The creaking got louder and louder, and then a girl about fifteen years old appeared. She was holding a large brown box and breathing heavily.

"Oh, it's just you," said Rhonda, relieved.

The girl smiled. "People are clamoring for your books, Miss Remington. I had to get more from the basement. They're waiting for you to sign them."

"I can't come right now," said Rhonda, somewhat distracted. "I'm talking to my assistant."

The girl's face fell. "Your *assistant?*"

"Max, this is Darlene Davis," said Rhonda. The girl's eyes narrowed. "Delia. *Delia* Davis."

Max nodded. "Hi."

Delia ignored him and turned to Rhonda. "It's getting late, and it's almost time for the competition."

"We're in the middle of something important," said Rhonda. She sounded flustered. "You go ahead. I'll be there in a minute."

Delia looked hurt, but she did as she was told.

Once Delia was out of hearing range, Max asked Rhonda, "Was your purse ever out of your sight?"

Rhonda shook her head. "It's been with me all night. Someone must have slipped in the note when I wasn't looking. But there are so many people here, it could have been *anyone*."

SHE GOT A LITTLE MAD

Rhonda looked at her watch. "Let's go up to the second floor. They're holding a reception there before the competition."

Max folded the note and slid it into his coat pocket.

Rhonda led Max up a flight of stairs and through a door into a huge room lit with chandeliers. Dozens of chairs were set up in neat rows in the center of the room, and over to the right were four windows that reached from the floor to the ceiling and had red velvet curtains.

Between two windows stood large wooden doors leading to a balcony. The doors were open. Through them you could see the dark woods behind Waldon Hall.

"What did you mean by a competition?" asked Max. "I thought you said you were being inducted into the Hall of Fame tonight."

"Wow, take a *look* at this place," said Larry, suddenly appearing next to Max. "Starchy had an adventure in a mansion just like this." He shook his head. "It didn't end well."

"What are you doing here?" asked Max, surprised to see his uncle.

Rhonda looked confused. "What do you mean 'what am I doing here'?"

Max kept forgetting that other people couldn't see or hear Larry.

"I couldn't stop thinking about this case," said Larry, "so I told Gertrude I'd take her to the movies next week."

"Max?" asked Rhonda.

Larry shrugged. "She got a little mad and kicked me. *Twice*. But I'll make it up to her. Maybe I'll bring her some jujubes."

Rhonda leaned in. *"Hello?"*

Max turned back to Rhonda. "Sorry, Miss Remington. I meant, what are you doing here — for the competition?"

IT WAS A TIE!

"The Mystery Hall of Fame committee reads hundreds of books," said Rhonda, "then narrows down their selections to ten authors."

"Holy cow!" said Larry. "I can barely get through one book." Max frowned at his uncle, hoping he'd clue in and be quiet.

"But I love *Starchy* comics! I have thirty. Right, Max?"

Max stepped in front of Larry, turning his back to him.

"From those ten," continued Rhonda, "they choose the final winner. But this year something unusual happened. Another author and I received *exactly* the same number of votes. Can you believe it?"

"It was a tie!" said Larry so loud that Max instinctively turned and said, "*Shh*."

Rhonda frowned.

Max tried to cover. "S-s-sure."

Larry looked at Max. "When did you start stuttering?"

"The committee came up with a brilliant solution," said Rhonda, "that would also attract tons of fans. They invited us both here tonight to tell our favorite stories. Three judges will vote on the best one. By the end of the night, one of us will be inducted into the Mystery Hall of Fame."

CHAPTER 3

SHE'D KILL ME — IF I WEREN'T ALREADY DEAD

"Who's the other author?" asked Max.

Rhonda pointed across the room to a lady standing beside a potted plant. "That's her over there. Nella Norman."

Max recognized the name. He'd read a few Nella Norman mysteries. They were good, but he liked Rhonda Remington's books better. This was the first time Max had ever seen Nella in person. She was wearing a flowing green dress and very high heels with shiny metal clasps on the straps.

Larry whistled and stepped out from behind Max. "She's a looker. A heck of a lot prettier than Gertrude."

Max motioned for Larry to be quiet.

"Don't tell Gertrude I said that. She'd kill me — if I weren't already dead."

A waiter came by and held out a tray. "Would you care for some cherry punch?"

Rhonda reached for a glass. So did Larry.

Max grabbed the glass out of Larry's hand before anyone noticed it hovering in the air.

"Hey," said Larry. "I'm thirsty."

"Do you know the man standing with Miss Norman?" Max asked Rhonda.

"That's her agent, Lew Jacobs. Nella doesn't go anywhere without him. She's his most popular client and keeps him in business. He treats her like royalty."

Max noticed the waiter offering Nella and Lew the cherry punch. Nella took a glass, but Lew shook his head and waved both his hands.

Just then, a group of fans surrounded Rhonda and thrust books under her nose. "Can we have your autograph? We *love* your books."

As Rhonda got swept away by the crowd, Max saw Nella's agent, Lew, pick up his briefcase, look around nervously and sneak out of the room.

"He's up to something," Max whispered to his uncle.

"Yep, he's definitely up to something. Wait. Who are we talking about?"

"Lew Jacobs, Nella Norman's agent." Max started to follow him. "Come on."

AND *DON'T* YOU FORGET IT

Just as they got to the door, Delia Davis blocked Max's way. Her eyes shot lasers at him.

"Excuse me," said Max, trying to get around her.

Delia blocked Max again. "*I'm* Rhonda's assistant."

"Sure," said Max, distracted. He peered over Delia's shoulder, trying not to lose sight of Lew Jacobs. He tried to get by Delia again, this time on her other side.

She put out her arm, blocking the doorway. "And *don't* you forget it."

"Uncle Larry, see where he goes!"

Delia frowned. "Who's Uncle Larry?"

"See where who goes?" asked Larry.

"The man with the briefcase!"

"What briefcase?" said Delia and Larry together.

Max looked directly at Delia. "Gotta go!" He slipped under her arm and ran into the hallway. Lew had vanished.

"He couldn't have gotten very far, Uncle Larry," said Max. "You check the rooms on the left, and I'll check the ones on the right."

"Hang on, Max. I've got an idea!"

Larry disappeared through the wall on

Max's left and came out at the other end of the hallway. "He's not in any of those rooms." Then he vanished into the wall on the right side. About halfway down the hallway, he stuck his head out through a door. "He's in here!"

CHAPTER 4

SWEET SUE GOT SCRATCHED

Max followed Larry into the room. It was a lounge filled with chairs, tables and a long brown couch by the window. Across from the couch was a television set. Lew snapped on the TV, then opened his briefcase and pulled out a piece of paper. He lifted a cell phone out of his pocket and punched in some numbers.

"That's a racing form he's holding, Max!" said Larry, sitting on the arm of the couch. "He's betting on horses."

"Two hundred dollars on Sweet Sue to win," said Lew.

Larry stretched out along the top of the couch. "This reminds me of one of the *Starchy* comics. The bad guy went to the racetrack with his pal, Jerome. They put laxatives into all of the horses' food — except for the horse they wanted to win. When the race started, the horses kept stopping to poop — and the bad guy's horse won!"

Max walked farther into the room.

Suddenly, Lew shouted, "What do you mean you can't take my bet?!"

There was a silence, and then Lew said, "I *know* I owe you money from the last race — *and* the one before that. But I've got a good feeling about Sweet Sue. Come on, Frank. You know I'm good for it."

Larry shook his head. "Don't give it to him, Frank."

Lew's face scrunched into a worried look. Then, a second later, his lips curled into a smile. "Thanks, Frank. I owe you one." He patted his forehead with a tissue. "So, that's two hundred on Sweet Sue." A second later, his smile disappeared. "Sweet Sue got scratched? But she was the 10 to 1 favorite! I can't believe it! If it wasn't for bad luck, I'd have no luck at all."

Just then, Lew spotted Max. "Hey, kid, come over here. Pick one … any one." He stuck out the racing form.

Larry looked at the form along with Max. "Tell him to pick Lady Godiva. She rode a horse, too!"

"Lady Godiva," said Max.

Lew repeated the name into the phone. "Yes … two hundred to win." He ended his call and tucked the phone into his pocket. "Maybe you'll bring me luck, kid. I sure could use some."

Larry slid down on the couch next to Lew's briefcase. "You brought *me* luck, Max. I'm a detective again!"

Max slipped into a nearby armchair. "Having a client as a finalist for the Mystery Hall of Fame sounds pretty lucky to me."

"You're right," said Lew, brightening. "If Nella wins the competition, sales of her books will soar through the roof! And I take a cut of every sale she makes. It's an agent's dream."

"Is Nella a good storyteller?" asked Max.

"She's great. But Rhonda is telling one of her best stories tonight. I've heard her tell it before, with special effects. It's going to be a tight race, but to be honest, I think Rhonda's better. Don't *ever* tell Nella I said that or she'll *kill* me."

"Author kills agent," said Larry. "Now *that's* a case I've never had."

I *HATE* PICKLES

Lew reached into his briefcase and lifted out a bottle of water. Then he peeled some

foil wrap that was around a large sandwich.
"Pastrami on rye," he said with a grin.
"Don't like the fussy food they serve at
these events."

Max glanced at the half-opened briefcase.
Lew noticed and pulled out a pickle. "Care
for a snack?"

"Ugh, I *hate* pickles," said Larry.

Max shook his head. "No, thanks."

"They're at the gate!" said the announcer
on the TV.

Lew's eyes shot to the screen. "Come on,
Lady Godiva!" He patted his forehead with
the tissue again.

Max and Larry walked out of the lounge.
As soon as he was out the door, Max stopped.

He took his notebook and pencil out of
his pocket and wrote …

Suspect #1 — Lew Jacobs
Motive — Gambling

"Lew Jacobs likes to gamble, and from what I overheard, he owes a lot of money. If Lew's planning the dirty trick on Rhonda, it would help his client Nella Norman win the competition, and Nella's book sales will go way up."

"Right!" said Larry. "And that'll put money in Lew Jacobs's pocket!"

CHAPTER 5

MY FOOL OF AN AGENT

When Max and Larry walked back to the reception, Max spotted Delia straightening some books on a table. Rhonda and Nella were standing next to her, talking. Max noticed that Nella kept looking over her shoulder, but he couldn't tell what, or who, she was looking at.

"So, Rhonda's a good writer?" Larry asked.

Max nodded. "One of the best mystery writers I've read. She'd make a great detective."

Larry's face fell. "Unlike me."

"No. That's not what I meant, Uncle Larry. I'm sure you were a great detective, with lots of challenging cases."

"You bet they were. I was once hired to go undercover as a ballet dancer."

"A *ballet* dancer?"

"Yeah. Someone was stealing all the tutus, and I was hired to discover who it was."

"Who was it?"

"Never did find out. Before I could investigate, I kicked myself in the head and fell off the stage. Doctor said I could have been *killed*. Then where would I be?"

"Dead?"

"Exactly."

Rhonda spotted Max and motioned for him to come over.

Max and Larry walked over to her. "Max, this is Nella —"

Before Rhonda could finish her sentence, Nella said a quick "Excuse me" and rushed off.

"How rude!" said Rhonda and Larry at the same time.

Max rushed off after Nella. He wormed his way through the crowd of people and finally spotted Nella by the balcony doors. He moved in close enough to hear her say to a waiter, "These doors are supposed to stay *open*. I was assured that they would be open the entire evening."

The waiter said that someone had complained about feeling a bit cold.

"Too bad," snapped Nella. "Tell them to put on a sweater."

"Yes, ma'am," said the waiter.

"I'm counting on you to make sure these doors remain open."

Nella made her way back to Rhonda, and Max followed. He wondered if the doors had something to do with the dirty trick that was going to be played on Rhonda.

"Sorry about that, Rhonda," said Nella. "What were you saying?"

"I — I was just introducing you to my young assistant. Max, this is Nella Norman, a marvelous writer and my competition tonight. Nella, this is Max Monroe."

Delia scowled at Max. More fans crowded around Rhonda, holding out copies of her books and begging her to autograph them.

"I should have brought some of *my* novels," said Nella to Max. "My fool of an agent didn't even suggest it."

Larry leaned in. "Your fool of an agent's too busy betting on horses."

Nella looked around the room. "Where is Lew, anyway?"

"I saw him in the lounge," said Max.

"What's he doing in there?"

Max wasn't sure if Nella knew about her agent's gambling, so he just said, "Eating a pickle."

A NEW QUEEN OF MYSTERIES

"Are you nervous about tonight's storytelling,

Miss Norman?" asked Max.

"A little. When you're telling a story, people have to use their imaginations. Personally, I don't think people *have* imaginations anymore." Someone waved from across the room. Nella pasted on a smile and waved back. "To help them along, I have a surprise that the audience and the judges are going to *love*."

Before Max could ask what the surprise was, a waiter passed by with a tray of mini tarts. Larry reached for the last lemon tart at the same time as Nella, but Nella grabbed it first.

"Darn," said Larry.

Max was glad his uncle hadn't gotten the tart. A flying tart would be hard to explain. But then Larry lifted an apple tart and scarfed it down. Max shot him a look.

The waiter's eyes opened wide. "How'd you do that, Miss Norman?"

"Do what?"

"Make that tart disappear."

Uh-oh, thought Max.

Nella looked at the tart she was holding. "What *are* you talking about?"

"How'd you make the *apple* tart disappear?" said the waiter.

Nella was getting annoyed. "I'm not a magician. I'm a storyteller."

Lew Jacobs came into the room and headed over to his client. "Ready to become the new Hall of Famer, Nella?"

"You bet I am," she sniffed. "I've been waiting my whole life for this honor, and *nothing's* going to stop me."

Lew smiled. "It's time for a new Queen of Mysteries — and *you'll* soon be wearing the crown."

Max turned and walked away. Larry joined him just as he was taking out his notebook.

Suspect #2 — Nella Norman
Motive — Winning the competition

"Nella really wants to win, and she's not going to let anything stop her," said Max. "If she's the one planning the dirty trick on Rhonda, it's to make sure her own story comes out on top."

"Right!" said Larry. "And that way she'll *guarantee* her place in the Mystery Hall of Fame."

CHAPTER 6

A CONFESSION

Max and Larry passed by the food table. "Look at these tiny sandwiches, Max! They're so cute."

The table was covered with trays of mini cucumber-and-cream-cheese sandwiches cut into pinwheels. Larry reached for one.

"Uncle *Larry*," hissed Max.

Larry popped a sandwich into his mouth.

As Max turned to see if anyone had

noticed, he found himself face-to-face with Delia.

"Just a friendly reminder — *I'm* Rhonda's assistant."

As quickly as she had appeared, Delia disappeared into the crowd.

"What's got her knickers in a knot?" asked Larry.

Max went looking for Delia. He found her at a table taking some blank name tags out of a bag and he sat down next to her. He had a confession. "I'm not really Rhonda's assistant."

"I know you're not!" said Delia. "So why does she keep telling people you *are*?"

"I … I can't say right now."

"Fine. Don't tell me. But I'll figure it out. I always do."

Delia started writing out the name tags. Her stomach growled. "Sorry. I haven't eaten all day."

"There are cucumber-and-cream-cheese sandwiches on the food table," said Max. "Would you like me to get you some?"

"I'd like you to get *lost*," snapped Delia. "Adios. And don't come back."

"She's nasty," said Larry, appearing in front of them. "Say something nice to calm her down."

Delia wrote out another name tag.

"You're working really hard tonight helping Rhonda," said Max. "How long have you been her assistant?"

Delia relaxed a little. "Actually, I'm assisting her just for this event. When word went out to the local fan club that

Rhonda needed help with her special effects, I volunteered. I'm the *president* of our chapter, you know. I write newsletters, handle her fan mail, send off autographed photos ..." Delia's face clouded over. "But when I was introduced to her this afternoon, she didn't even know who I *was*. Can you believe it? And on top of that — she hasn't gotten my name right once. I'm not sure if I even *want* her to win anymore."

I LOVE SURPRISES!

Two women approached the table, each holding a small clipboard. One was wearing a red jacket and black pants, the other a blue dress. They stepped right through Larry. "We're the judges," said one of the women. "We were told you had our name tags."

"And don't forget me!" said a man wearing a blue suit and a yellow bow tie. He popped a mini sandwich into his mouth. "I'll need one as well."

Delia gathered up the tags and handed them over. As she lifted her arm, Max noticed a scrap of paper on the tabletop with the three judges' names written on it. Delia's arm came back down and covered it again.

After the judges left, Max said, "Nella

Norman told me she's got a surprise planned that she knows the judges will love."

"I love surprises!" said Larry, rubbing his hands together.

"Pfft," sneered Delia. "Her *surprise* is a special effect. Both she and Rhonda are allowed to use special effects in their stories. Whatever it is, it won't be as good as Rhonda's."

"Who's taking care of Rhonda's special effects?" asked Max.

"I'll give you one guess," said Delia.

Larry's eyes widened. "Let me guess! Let me guess!"

"You?" said Max.

Delia looked proud. "Who else? *I'm* her assistant, remember?"

"Hey!" said Larry. "I didn't get a chance to guess."

Delia's lips curled into a smile. "I probably shouldn't tell you this."

Larry leaned on the table. "Your secret's safe with us."

Delia whispered into Max's ear so no one would overhear. "There's a part in Rhonda's story where a ghost wolf comes crashing through the wall. We have sound effects and everything. Rhonda brought along her husky dog that looks just like a *real* wolf."

"Where's the dog?" asked Max.

"He's in a crate outside the building. There's a rope tied to the crate door, and at exactly the right moment, I'll pull the rope. Once the door opens, the dog will dash out into the woods. It's going to be *awesome!*"

"How will you know when the right moment is?" asked Max.

Delia leaned back in her chair. "I'll be in a room directly under the balcony where Rhonda will be standing. When she gives the signal, I'll hear her through the window."

"Sounds amazing," said Max. "I'm sure Rhonda appreciates everything you're doing to help her."

Delia's eyes darkened. "She sure hasn't shown any appreciation since I got here. Every time I try to talk to her, she brushes me off."

At that moment, Lew Jacobs walked by their table. Delia turned to Max. "I don't trust him — or Nella Norman. When they first arrived and were setting up their effects, I overheard her tell her agent that they had to pull out every trick they had so she could win."

"You hear that, Max?" asked Larry. "Every *trick*! Maybe even a dirty one?"

Delia got up. "I'm going to go do a final check on Rhonda's special effects." She crumpled the paper she'd written the judges' names on and stuffed it into her skirt pocket.

Max looked at his uncle. "I wish I'd gotten a better look at Delia's handwriting."

Larry grinned. "Leave it to me."

He whooshed across the room and slid the note out of Delia's pocket. As it floated across the room, the same waiter who'd served the tarts saw it. His eyes almost popped out of his head.

AN OPEN-AND-SHUT CASE

"Is this what you wanted?" asked Larry.

Max grabbed the paper. The waiter rushed over to him. "How'd you *do* that?" he asked.

Larry grinned. "Tell him you have a friend who's a ghost."

Max gulped. "A magician never reveals his secrets."

The waiter nodded sadly. "I know. I know. Care for a butter tart?"

"Thanks," said Larry, grabbing one and gobbling it down.

"Wow," said the waiter. "You're *good*."

He shook his head as he walked off. Once the waiter was out of earshot, Max turned to his uncle. "You've got to stop *doing* that."

"Doing what?"

Max shook his head. "Never mind."

He smoothed out the crumpled paper and looked at it. The three judges' names were written on it.

Leslie Branson
Thomas Carter
Alice Dane

"What are you looking for, Max?" asked Larry.

"I want to compare Delia's handwriting to the handwriting on Rhonda's note." Max pulled the note out of his pocket and placed it next to the paper. "The handwriting's the *same*, Uncle Larry."

"Then *Delia's* the one who's going to play the dirty trick on Rhonda tonight!

We've solved the case!" Larry did a happy dance.

"It doesn't make sense," whispered Max.

Larry stopped dancing. "What doesn't? It's an open-and-shut case."

"If Delia's planning to play the trick on Rhonda, why slip her a note *warning* her?"

Larry's shoulders slumped. "I guess you're right. If you're planning on robbing someone, you don't go telling them ahead of time." Then he had a second thought. "Unless …"

"Unless what?" asked Max.

"Unless Delia only wanted Rhonda to *think* someone was going to play a trick on her."

"Good point, Uncle Larry."

Max took out his notebook and wrote …

Suspect #3 — Delia Davis
Motive — Sabotage

"Delia's been upset with Rhonda all night for not appreciating the amount of work she's done for her. She's the president of Rhonda's local fan club, but Rhonda didn't even know who she was. *And* Rhonda hasn't been very nice to her from what I've seen. By writing the note, Delia might be trying to worry Rhonda so much that she won't do her best storytelling and lose the competition."

"Right!" said Larry. "That'll teach Rhonda a lesson."

CHAPTER 7

SNOW ... IN JULY?

A woman with straight red hair and even redder lips stepped to the front of the room. "May I have your attention please." The excited chatter died down. "I'm Cordelia Conrad, president of the Mystery Hall of Fame. Please take your seats. The competition is about to begin!"

People made their way to the chairs and quieted down.

"Our first storyteller," said Mrs. Conrad, "is Nella Norman. The story she's chosen to tell this evening is called 'The Snow Ghost Mystery.'"

Everyone clapped as Nella stepped to the front of the room. In a dramatic voice she began telling the story of a family who was sent a mysterious invitation to spend their Christmas holidays in a cabin in the woods. When they arrived at the cabin, they were surprised to find an old woman living there. She knew everything about them — even though they'd never met before. Nella was a really good storyteller, and everybody listened so intently that you could have heard a pin drop. Near the end of the story, she told of a howling snowstorm that blew in on Christmas Eve. At that very moment, everyone in the audience was shocked to see snow *actually* falling outside the balcony doors of Waldon Hall! People gasped and pointed when they saw it.

Larry's eyebrows went up. "Snow … in July?" He whooshed out of the room through the open balcony doors. A few seconds later, he whooshed back inside beside Max. "Some guy's working a snow machine on the roof. *Brilliant*."

Max noticed that Lew Jacobs looked thrilled with the audience's response.

At the end of the story, everybody clapped and cheered. The judges looked *really* impressed. Nella smiled proudly and bowed several times.

Mrs. Conrad made an announcement that there would be a ten-minute intermission before the next story. Max knew he was running out of time.

TOO MUCH CHERRY PUNCH

As people moved around, Max overheard Lew ask a waiter for directions to the men's room. "I drank too much cherry punch," he said, laughing.

Max looked around and spotted Nella talking to her fans. Rhonda was in the corner, wringing her hands. "Miss Remington looks really worried," he said to Larry.

"She should be. Nella Norman's story was terrific!"

Rhonda made her way over to them. "Oh, Max, have you figured out who's planning the trick?"

"Not yet, but I'm working on it."

Delia appeared and whispered to Rhonda, "I'll go downstairs and get ready for your special effects."

Rhonda nodded.

"Nella's story was really something, wasn't it?" continued Delia. "And that snow was a fantastic special effect."

This was the last thing Rhonda needed to hear. "Oh, dear," she said, rubbing her forehead.

"Don't worry, Miss Remington," said Delia. "I'm sure *everything* will go great with your story, too."

"Thank you, Diane."

Delia's mouth got all pinched. "Delia. *Delia* Davis."

Rhonda looked flustered. "Oh, yes, of course, dear."

Delia spun around and almost knocked down Nella Norman as they both headed toward the door.

CHAPTER 8

THE MYSTERIOUS CREATURE

Exactly ten minutes later, Cordelia Conrad made an announcement for everyone to take their seats. Lew and several people came in from the hallway. Then Nella came in and walked over to a seat in the front row. When everyone had sat down, Mrs. Conrad said, "And now it's time for this evening's second story. It's called 'The Mystery of Stone Wolf,' and our storyteller is Rhonda Remington!"

Everyone clapped.

Rhonda took a deep breath, walked to the front of the room and began her story.

"Every year, at exactly nine o'clock on the ninth day of the ninth month, *everyone* in the village of Dunbarton locked their doors, turned out their lights … and *hid*. Hid from what, you ask?" Rhonda moved closer to the audience. "There was a legend, passed down from generation to generation, about a mysterious creature that, night after night, attacked the farmers' sheep. The people of the village held a meeting and decided to lay traps all around the fields. That night, at exactly nine o'clock, a wolf was caught in one of the traps.

"But before the villagers could get to the wolf, a landslide thundered down the mountain and buried it *alive*. The next day, more sheep were attacked. The villagers had caught the wrong animal! The mysterious creature was still out there. Legend has it that the innocent wolf's spirit entered one of the stones that had crushed the wolf, and that *same* stone was the first one used to build ... this ... very ... building."

Rhonda's voice got deeper. "Once a year, at the stroke of nine, the spirit of the innocent wolf *escapes* from the wall to seek revenge on the descendants of those who laid the trap." Rhonda looked right into the eyes of her listeners. "Tonight ... is that night!"

The clock on the wall suddenly chimed. Everyone looked up. It was *exactly* nine o'clock.

Rhonda rushed across the room, motioning for people to join her on the balcony. Everyone scrambled from their seats and raced after her. "Come on, Max!" shouted Larry, getting caught up in the excitement.

Max followed but kept his eyes on Nella and her agent.

Rhonda leaned over the railing and shouted, "It's happening NOW!"

The clock continued to chime ... *three* ... *four* ... *five* ... Growling filled the air. *Six* ... *seven* ... The growling got louder and louder. *Eight* ... And then — on the ninth chime — the sound of crashing stones *blasted* through the night air.

Everyone gasped. People pushed and shoved to see down to the ground. They

held their breath and waited for the wolf
to come hurling through the wall. With
wide eyes, they saw … a cute brown rabbit.
It hopped over the fake snow and into the
dark woods.

The audience burst out laughing. Nella
and her agent laughed the loudest. The
judges looked confused, but soon they were
laughing, too. Rhonda stood there, stunned.
She couldn't believe what had happened.

Max bolted out of the room, down the
stairs and out the back door of Waldon Hall.

CHAPTER 9

A PICKY EATER

The fake snow that had come down
during Nella Norman's story covered the
ground. Max spotted some footprints
and quickly followed them over to the
crate that the rabbit had escaped from.
A black blanket covered it, and the door
was wide open. Inside, on the floor, was
a mangled sandwich with a huge bite
taken out of it.

Max leaned in to get a better look.
The sandwich rose in midair and

Larry appeared, holding it. He took a bite.

"*What are you doing?!*" shouted Max.

"Mmm, mustard … my favorite!"

"You can't eat the evidence!"

"Okay. Okay." Larry dropped the sandwich. "It was soggy, anyway."

Max bent down to examine it. "I wonder what a sandwich is doing in a dog crate."

Larry's eyes lit up. "I know! Rhonda wanted to make sure her dog didn't get hungry while he waited for her to tell her story."

"You could be right, Uncle Larry. But why a sandwich? Why not dog food?"

"Maybe the dog is a picky eater?"

A SWITCHEROO

Max walked around the crate and spotted the rope tied to the door handle. He followed it as it went up the wall and through an open window. "This rope must lead to the room Delia's in."

"What did she say she needed the rope for?" asked Larry.

"When Rhonda got to the part in her story where the wolf crashes through the stone wall, Delia was supposed to pull open the crate door with the rope and let the dog run out."

"Well, somebody did a switcheroo."

Max nodded. "And now we know what the dirty trick is. We just need to find out *who* did the switch."

Max moved around and noticed the rabbit tracks that went from the crate through the fake snow.

"I had a rabbit named Rumpy when I was a kid," said Larry. "Brought him to school one day for show-and-tell."

He reached for the sandwich again.

"Leave it alone," said Max.

"Rumpy took off at recess. Harry and I chased him all around the school yard, but he got away." Larry burst out crying. "I never saw him again! *Poor* Rumpy — all alone in the world!"

"I'm sure he was okay, Uncle Larry."

Larry kept blubbering.

"Uncle Larry, we're in the middle of a case." Larry still didn't stop. "And I need your help."

Larry looked at Max. "You do?"

"The window's too high for me to look inside." Max pointed at the window above the crate. "Would you go up and look. Tell me if you see anything?"

Larry wiped his eyes. "Sure." He sniffled then floated up to the window and peered in. "I see the end of the rope, Max."

"You don't see Delia?"

"No," said Larry. "She must have run upstairs when she heard all the fuss."

"Do you see anything unusual?" asked Max.

Larry stuck his head right through the window. "A sandwich!" His head came back out. "Maybe it's the same kind as the one in the crate. I'll go see if it has mustard on it."

Larry flew through the window. A second

later, he flew back out, licking his fingers.
"Nope. It's cucumber and cream cheese.
But that doesn't mean she didn't do it."

Max crouched down and examined
the footprints that led to the crate. They

were clear, until the area right in front of the crate door. At that point they got all jumbled up. Some dog prints were visible in the fake snow, leading away from the crate. "Somebody led Rhonda's dog out of the crate," said Max.

Larry leaned over to look. "You're right, Max. And they went that way." He pointed to the pathway that led to the parking lot.

Max took one last look at the crate, the footprints, the rope and the sandwich — then he stood up.

"I know who played the trick on Rhonda."

CHAPTER 10

MAX SOLVES THE CASE

Max asked Delia, Nella, Lew and a still-upset Rhonda to join him behind Waldon Hall. "Earlier today, Miss Remington called me, asking for help. Someone had slipped a note in her purse that said, *Beware ... a dirty trick!*" Max held up the note.

Delia, Nella and Lew looked at each other awkwardly.

"The person who wrote the note was trying to warn Miss Remington," continued

Max, "and that person was you, Delia."

Delia looked surprised.

"Your handwriting on the list of judges' names matches the writing on the note. You're the local president of the Rhonda Remington fan club, and you've been helping her all night. But Miss Remington hasn't thanked you once for all your hard work. Maybe you slipped her the note to worry her, hoping that she would be too distracted to tell a great story."

"I *was* upset, but I didn't actually want her to *lose*," said Delia. "I'm her biggest fan!"

"Exactly," said Max. "You care about her, so when you overheard Nella Norman tell her agent that they had to pull out every trick to win, you slipped Miss Remington the note to warn her."

"That's right. Miss Remington might not have believed me if I had told her in person," said Delia. "I *knew* Nella and her agent were up to something."

NOT ENOUGH TIME

Max walked closer to the crate, then turned to Nella. "Miss Norman, you really wanted to win the competition tonight. You even told your agent that *nothing* would stop you from winning. You put a lot of work into your story and special effects, and wanted to make sure it landed you a spot in the Hall of Fame."

"Yes, I admit I want to be the new Queen of Mysteries," said Nella, "but I want to win fair and square."

"The fake snow you used in your story

was a big help in solving the mystery," said Max. "If it weren't for the snow, these footprints wouldn't be visible. The shape of the prints was clearly made by a flat shoe, and you're wearing high heels. I remembered noticing their shiny clasps when I first saw you.

"There was only a ten-minute break after your story," continued Max, "and you were talking to people for most of it. There wasn't enough time for you to change your shoes, switch the animals and still get back in time for Miss Remington's story."

Nella pointed a finger at Max. "*You* are a genius."

Larry beamed. "I taught him *everything* he knows."

YOU HAVE *NO* PROOF

Max turned to Lew Jacobs. "That leaves you, Mr. Jacobs."

Lew's eyes darted around nervously.

"You like betting on horse races, and you owe a lot of money. If your client Nella Norman was inducted into the Hall of Fame, there would be lots of publicity and lots of book sales. As her agent, you get a percentage of those sales — and that would add up to quite a bit of money. You *had* to make sure Rhonda *didn't* win."

"And just *when* would I have had time to switch the animals?" asked Lew.

"During the ten-minute break between stories."

"I went to the bathroom during the

break! You can ask the waiter I spoke to!"

"I heard you tell the waiter you needed to go to the bathroom because you drank too much cherry punch. But you haven't been drinking cherry punch all night. You *pretended* to go to the bathroom, then you snuck down here, took the dog out and replaced him with the rabbit."

"Sorry to interrupt, Max," said Rhonda. "My dog's friendly, but he would have barked as soon as he saw Lew."

"Mr. Jacobs was prepared for that," responded Max. "He couldn't risk attracting attention, so he distracted the dog with a sandwich."

Lew crossed his arms. "You have *no* proof that was my sandwich."

A *HORRIBLE* THING TO DO

Max continued. "There were only cream-cheese sandwiches at the reception. But this one has mustard on it. Whoever played the trick must have brought this sandwich. Mr. Jacobs, earlier tonight you were eating a pastrami sandwich in the lounge. You told me you always bring your own food to these events. I'll bet that if we had a look in your briefcase —"

"My briefcase is locked, and I can't find the key," said Lew.

Larry grinned. "I've got this covered." He popped open the briefcase and tilted it. Some foil sandwich wrap with a streak of mustard on it fell out. So did a leash.

"Well, look at that," said Larry.

Max picked up the sandwich wrap and

the leash and turned to Rhonda. "Your dog was too busy eating the sandwich to bark. That also made it easier to lead him away with this leash."

Max turned to Lew. "Mr. Jacobs, you're definitely the one who played this trick on Miss Remington."

Lew hung his head. He looked truly sorry for what he'd done. "It was a *horrible* thing to do to you, Rhonda, but I've lost a *ton* of money. My gambling's gotten out of hand, and I was desperate! When I heard that you were telling this story, I made a plan to bring a rabbit and switch the animals. I'm really, really sorry."

Rhonda patted Lew on the back. "It *was* a terrible thing to do, Lew. But if you tell me where my dog is, I'll forgive you."

Lew gave her a little smile. "He's in my car. Safe and sound."

As everyone walked back into Waldon Hall, Larry gave Max a wink and a big thumbs-up.

CONGRATULATIONS

Because of everything that had happened, the Hall of Fame committee decided to cancel that night's ceremony. They would hold a second competition with new judges to give Rhonda and Nella a fair chance.

Over the next week, Grandpa Harry, Max and Larry each read a Rhonda Remington mystery while they waited to hear who the winner would be.

When the night of the competition rolled around, Rhonda called to give Max the scoop. She had been chosen for the Mystery Hall of Fame!

"I couldn't have done it without you, Max," Rhonda told him. "Thank you for all your help."

"Congratulations, Miss Remington!" said Max. "I knew you could do it."

Max shared the good news with Harry and Larry. They celebrated with a fresh box of Mighty Moe's Donuts!

SPOT THE DIFFERENCE

Detectives have to be observant.
Can you find five differences between these
two pictures?

1. Harry's eyebrows are missing.
2. The windowpanes are gone.
3. The soda bottle on the right has a different label.
4. Max's teeth are missing.
5. Larry's flashlight is gone.

EVERYONE LOVES THE GHOST AND MAX MONROE!

Praise for Case #1

"A ghostly (but not scary) new chapter-book mystery series kicks off … Falcone keeps readers guessing and pages turning with humorous dialogue and a quickly paced plot."
— *Kirkus Reviews*

"This beginning chapter book will engage youngsters who like mysteries mixed with silly characters."
— *School Library Journal*

Praise for Case #2

"Falcone crafts a compelling mystery title just right for newly independent readers … Introduce Max to budding detectives or children who like to laugh as they read."
— *Kirkus Reviews*

"The solid mystery, complete with clues, red herrings and several suspects, is paired with humorous dialogue, chuckle-worthy puns and clever asides."
— *School Library Journal*

**The Ghost and Max Monroe
Case #1: The Magic Box**
L. M. Falcone
HC 978-1-77138-153-6
$12.95 US • $12.95 CDN
PB 978-1-77138-017-1
$6.95 US • $6.95 CDN

**The Ghost and Max Monroe
Case #2: The Missing Zucchini**
L. M. Falcone
HC 978-1-77138-154-3
$12.95 US • $12.95 CDN
PB 978-1-77138-018-8
$6.95 US • $6.95 CDN